D1256238

Say Please!

The Sound of PL

By Alice K. Flanagan

The Child's World®

Marysville Public Library
231 South Plum Street
Marysville, Ohio 43040
937-642-1876

When you ask for something, say please. It can mean a lot— you will see.

Would you please
let me play?

Please, can my friend stay?

Please wash your hands
before you eat.

10

Please pass the meat.

Please put away
the saucers and plates.

13

14

Please, would you let
me use your skates?

Please cover your mouth
when you sneeze.

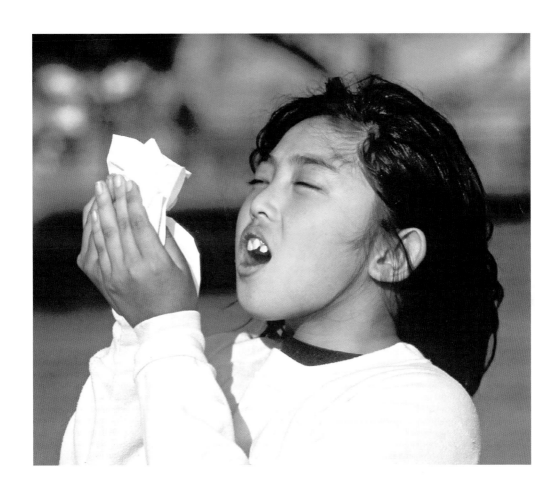

18

Water the plants,
would you please?

Saying "please" makes such a difference.

Word List

plants

plates

play

please

plus

Note to Parents and Educators

Welcome to Wonder Books® Phonics Readers! These books are based on current research that supports the idea that our brains detect patterns rather than apply rules. This means that children learn to read more easily when they are taught the familiar spelling patterns found in English. As children progress in their reading, they can use these spelling patterns to figure out more complex words.

The Phonics Readers texts provide the opportunity to practice and apply knowledge of the sounds in natural language. The ten books on the long and short vowels introduce the sounds using familiar onsets and *rimes*, or spelling patterns, for reinforcement. The letter(s) before the vowel in a word are considered the onset. Changing the onset allows the consonant books in the series to maintain the practice and reinforcement of the rimes. The repeated use of a word or phrase reinforces the target sound.

As an example, the word "cat" might be used to present the short "a" sound, with the letter "c" being the onset and "–at" being the rime. This approach provides practice and reinforcement for the short "a" sound, since there are many familiar words with the "–at" rime.

The number on the spine of each book facilitates arranging the books in the order in which the sounds are learned. The books can also be arranged into groups of long vowels, short vowels, consonants, and blends. All the books in each grouping have their numbers printed in the same color on the spine. The books can be grouped and regrouped easily and quickly, depending on the teacher's needs.

The stories and accompanying photographs in this series are based on time-honored concepts in children's literature: Well-written, engaging texts and colorful, high-quality photographs combine to produce books that children want to read again and again.

Dr. Peg Ballard
Minnesota State University, Mankato, MN

About the Author

Alice K. Flanagan taught elementary school for ten years. Now she writes for children and teachers. She has been writing for more than twenty years. Some of her books include biographies, phonics books, holiday books, and information books about careers, animals, and weather. Alice K. Flanagan lives with her husband in Chicago, Illinois.

Published by The Child's World®
PO Box 326
Chanhassen, MN 55317-0326
800-599-READ
www.childsworld.com

Photo Credits
© Ariel Skelly/Corbis: 18
© Barbara Stitzer/PhotoEdit: 14
© David Young Wolff/PhotoEdit: 9, 17
© Ed Bock/Corbis: 2d
© Jose Luis Pelaez,Inc./Corbis: 5
© Michael Newman/PhotoEdit: 6
© Myrleen Ferguson Cate/PhotoEdit: 10
© Nancy Sheehen/PhotoEdit: cover
© Royalty-Free/Corbis: 13
© Tony Freeman/PhotoEdit: 21

The Child's World®: Mary Berendes, Publishing Director
Editorial Directions, Inc.: E. Russell Primm, Editorial Director and Line Editor;
Alice K. Flanagan/Flanagan Publishing Services, Photo Researcher, Linda S. Koutris, Photo Selector

Copyright © 2004 by The Child's World®
All rights reserved. No part of this book may be
reproduced or utilized in any form or by any means
without written permission from the publisher.
Printed in the United States of America.

Library of Congress Cataloging-in-Publication Data
Flanagan, Alice K.
  Say please! : the sound of PL / by Alice K. Flanagan.
    p. cm. — (Wonder books)
Summary: Simple text features words that contain the consonant blend, "pl."
  ISBN 1-59296-158-4 (Library Bound : alk. paper)
  [1. English language—Phonetics. 2. Reading.] I. Title. II. Series:
Wonder books (Chanhassen, Minn.)
PZ7.F59824Say 2004
[E—dc22
                        2003018103

24